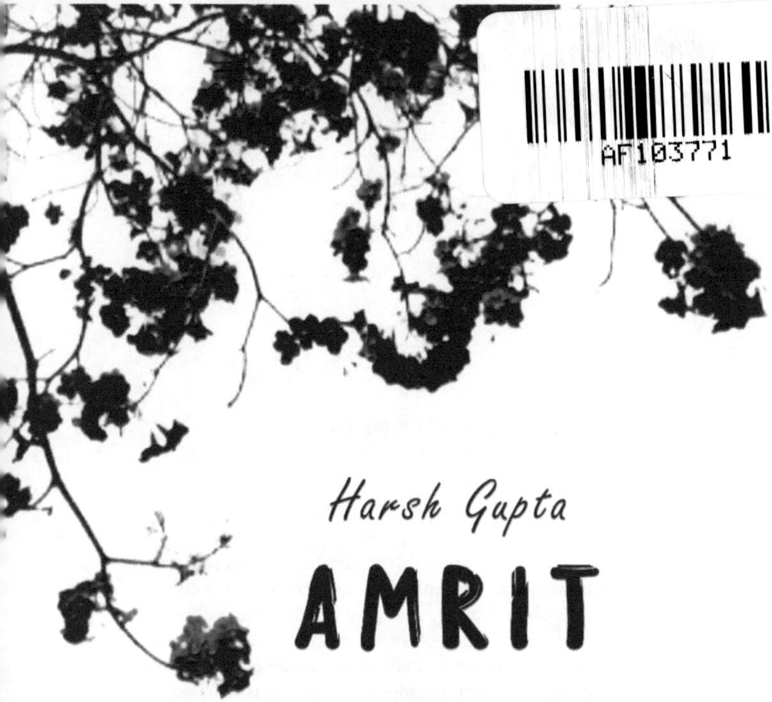

Harsh Gupta

AMRIT
KI
RUH

NewDelhi • London

BLUEROSE PUBLISHERS
India | U.K.

Copyright © Harsh Gupta 2025

All rights reserved by author. No part of this publication may be reproduced, stored in a retrieval system or transmitted in any form or by any means, electronic, mechanical, photocopying, recording or otherwise, without the prior permission of the author. Although every precaution has been taken to verify the accuracy of the information contained herein, the publisher assumes no responsibility for any errors or omissions. No liability is assumed for damages that may result from the use of information contained within.

BlueRose Publishers takes no responsibility for any damages, losses, or liabilities that may arise from the use or misuse of the information, products, or services provided in this publication.

For permissions requests or inquiries regarding this publication, please contact:

BLUEROSE PUBLISHERS
www.BlueRoseONE.com
info@bluerosepublishers.com
+91 8882 898 898
+4407342408967

ISBN: 978-93-7018-686-6

Cover design: Yash Singhal
Typesetting: Namrat Saini

First Edition: May 2025

Dedicated to:

The Patience,

The life,

रूह

Prologue

This's a short story on Amrit's Ruh, where he has described the beauty and the pain of patience at the same time. Amrit fought with himself to accept his feeling and to know how important is to accept what you feel.

How he used to dream about his life with Ruh and how there was that hidden happiness in everything about Ruh.

Amrit never born as poet, neither he learnt He's simply in love that he became one.

Contents

Chapter 1: The Beginning 1
Chapter 2: Becoming Friends 3
Chapter 3: The Walk 6
Chapter 4: Unspoken Feelings 9
Chapter 5: The Heartbreak 12
Chapter 6: The Decision 14
Chapter 7: The Confession 16
Chapter 8: The Stars & Moons 18
Chapter 9: The Meeting 20
Chapter 10: The Last Call 24
Chapter 11: Awaiting Destiny 27

CHAPTER 1
The Beginning

> must remember
> life is a journey filled with chaos
> it's a maze with endless possibilities
> - the beginning

Finally he called;

It started four years ago when Amrit met Ruh online. The world was gripped by the COVID-19 pandemic, and like many others, their lives had shifted to virtual spaces. Amrit, a second-year student, was still reeling from a broken friendship that had left him feeling isolated.

His first year at college hadn't been great, and the pandemic only added to his sense of disconnection.

Ruh, on the other hand, was a freshman, full of enthusiasm and ready to take on the world. She had joined the same college society as Amrit for a project, and despite the distance, her spirit shone through.

Unlike Amrit, Ruh had a long-distance relationship that she was committed to, bringing a sense of stability to her new college life.

Their first meeting was a typical online affair—video calls, chat messages, and shared documents. It wasn't love at first sight for Amrit. In fact, he knew nothing about Ruh beyond her cheerful aspect and dedication to the project. But as weeks turned into months, their interactions became more frequent, and a friendship began to form.

CHAPTER 2
Becoming Friends

> friendship - the relation
> which blossoms
> the flower of love

As the project progressed, Amrit and Ruh started working together regularly. They coordinated on tasks, brainstormed ideas, and gradually moved from discussing work to sharing bits of their personal lives.

Their conversations often stretched beyond the confines of the project. They discussed everything from their favorite books and movies to their dreams and aspirations.

Amrit found himself looking forward to their meetings, appreciating Ruh's enthusiasm and positivity.

Ruh's presence became a bright spot in Amrit's otherwise monotonous routine. Despite her own challenges—study pressure, family expectations, and a difficult environment—she managed to stay optimistic.

Amrit admired her strength and resilience, but he kept his growing feelings to himself, haunted by the remnants of his past.

Their friendship deepened with each passing day. They began to share personal stories and secrets.

Amrit confided in Ruh about his struggles with his studies and the pain of losing his closed one due to pandemic. Ruh, in turn, spoke about her long-distance relationship and the challenges of maintaining it. They bonded over their mutual understanding of each other's hardships.

One evening, after a particularly inspiring brainstorming session, Amrit found himself unable to sleep. His mind was filled with thoughts of Ruh, and before he knew it, he had written a poem, channeling his emotions into words. He kept the poem to himself, using it as a way to process his feelings.

"tu kisi samudra si hai

mai kisi ret sa

is khwabon ki duniya ka dastoor to dekh

tu meri aur mai tujhme sama gaya"

- khwaab

Amrit started noticing little things about Ruh that he hadn't before.

The way her eyes sparkled when she talked about something she was passionate about, her infectious laughter, and her unwavering determination. He admired her for her kindness and empathy, traits that made her stand out in a world that often seemed harsh and indifferent. That smile, for which he used to wait for days.

Despite his growing affection, Amrit was careful not to cross any boundaries. He valued their friendship too much to risk it by revealing his feelings prematurely.

He also respected Ruh's commitment to her boyfriend, recognizing that she was in a relationship that brought her stability and happiness.

Her happiness was the most important thing to Amrit, more than his feelings too.

CHAPTER 3
The Walk

> tujhe dekh ke mera hasna sahi
> tujhe dekh mera rona sahi
> bas tujhe dekhna
> aur dekhte rehna hi sahi;
>
> -nayan

In his final year, as the country began to reopen, physical classes resumed. Amrit was both excited and nervous to meet Ruh in person for the first time.

One day, outside the girls' hostel, he mustered the courage to ask her for a walk. They had been friends for so long that meeting in person felt like a natural progression, yet the anticipation made his heart race.

The walk was simple but significant. They strolled through the campus, talking about everything and nothing. Amrit was struck by how beautiful Ruh looked in person, and how familiar her presence felt. It was as if he had known her for years, even though they had only met online.

Amrit just silently listening each and every bit of Ruh's talk, as if he's lost into her.

For Amrit, it felt like a walk towards forever. He knew then that Ruh was the one he wanted to be with. But she was still in a relationship, and Amrit respected that.

He couldn't bring himself to disrupt her happiness. Instead, he focused on enjoying the moment, cherishing the time they spent together.

They walked past the library, the canteen, and the auditorium, each spot sparking memories of their online discussions. They laughed about the time they had argued over the best way to approach a project task and reminisced about the late-night brainstorming sessions that had brought them closer.

Amrit felt a deep sense of contentment, knowing that Ruh had become an integral part of his life.

As they walked, Amrit found himself stealing glances at Ruh, memorizing every detail of her face. He noticed the way the sunlight played on her hair, the smile which was one of a kind, and the warmth in her eyes.

Amrit wanted to hold onto these moments, to etch them into his memory forever.

>tere saath chalna hai
>tere saath udna hai
>tere saath baith do pal bitane hain
>chalna udna baithna mai kuch na jaanu
>jaanu to bas itna, ki tera hi saath zaroori
>-tera saath

CHAPTER 4
Unspoken Feelings

> tujhe dekh ke mera hasna sahi
> tujhe dekh mera rona sahi
> bas tujhe dekhna
> aur dekhte rehna hi sahi;
>
> -nayan

A year prior, during one of their casual conversations, Amrit had asked Ruh about her ideal partner. She had mentioned her boyfriend, a fact that was clear from her Instagram profile, which Amrit frequented though he never interfered. He saw her happy and in love, which made him question his own feelings.

As his final year progressed, Amrit's internal struggle intensified. He continued to hide his feelings, afraid of losing the friendship he cherished.

COVID had been particularly harsh on him, taking away his closed one, who had been his confidante.

The loss, combined with the strain of his studies and isolation from friends, weighed heavily on him. He often found solace in rereading old chats with Ruh and looking at their only picture together.

Their interactions were a lifeline for Amrit during those tough times. He appreciated Ruh's constant support and encouragement. She had a way of making him feel better, even on his worst days. Her optimism was contagious, and he often found himself smiling after their conversations.

Amrit began to realize that his feelings for Ruh were more than just a fleeting infatuation. He admired her for her strength and resilience, and he respected her for her honesty and kindness.

His feelings for her grew deeper with each passing day, but he was determined to keep them hidden.

He often found himself daydreaming about a future with Ruh. He imagined what it would be like to hold her hand, to share his dreams with her, and to build a life together. But these were just dreams, and he reminded himself that Ruh was already committed to someone else.

One sleepless night, Amrit decided to channel his feelings into writing. He poured his heart into a poem, expressing his unspoken emotions. Writing became his way of coping, of dealing with the pain of unrequited love. It was a silent confession, a way for him to acknowledge his feelings without disrupting their friendship.

> mai us mod pe hun
> zindagi ka hath thaame
> tu mujhe ek aawaz lagana
> teri kasam,
> tere us aawaz ke intazar se zinda hun
> tu mujhe us mod pe milna
> jahan bas mai aur tum hon
> meri mohabbat tere ishq ka intazaar karri
> -intazar

CHAPTER 5
The Heartbreak

> dil ki baat bas dil jaane
> haar ya jeet bas dil jaane
> tujhe khone ka gam bas dil jaane
> tere na hone ka gam bas dil jaane
> dil ke baat to bas dil hi jaane
> -tuta dil

One day, Amrit's intuition flared. He sensed something was wrong with Ruh and called her, "Kya hua? Sab theek hai? Mujhe kuch ajeeb lag raha hai. Agar tumhe kuch batana ho to bolna." Her reply was unexpected: "I broke up!"

Amrit was shocked and deeply saddened for Ruh. He knew how much her relationship had meant to her. While he consoled her, there was no one to console him as he cried for Ruh and the pain she was enduring. He yearned to be with her, but fear still held him back.

He listened as Ruh poured out her heart, sharing the details of the breakup and the pain she was going through. Amrit felt a deep sense of empathy for her.

He wanted to be there for her, to offer her the support and comfort she needed. But he also knew that he had to respect her space and give her time to heal.

Amrit's feelings for Ruh grew even stronger during this period. He admired her courage in dealing with the breakup and her determination to move forward.

He saw a different side of her, one that was vulnerable and in need of support. It made him realize just how much he cared for her.Despite his own pain, Amrit focused on being a good friend to Ruh. He offered her a listening ear, and words of encouragement.

He wanted her to know that she wasn't alone, that he was there for her no matter what. Their bond grew stronger as they navigated this difficult time together.

CHAPTER 6
The Decision

> jang jab dil aur dimag ki ho
> aksar dimag sahi hota
> aur dil bas sahi hona chahta
> aur fir dil jeet kar haar jata
> -jzang

Days turned into regular conversations. Amrit supported Ruh as best as he could while battling his own feelings. His heart ached to confess, but the fear of losing her friendship lingered.

There was this tension going on between his feeling and him, jung khudse khudki thi.

It was much difficult for Amrit to cope up with the real world at the same time, as the feeling was growing day by day but he was scared as his mind was again again implying towards a No from her end.

Finally, his heart won over his fears. Sometimes he was not able to understand his own feelings,

> sometimes you want
>
> no love no hope
>
> no magic no reason
>
> just the need to feel alive
>
> and i guess ruh you are my reason to feel alive

CHAPTER 7
The Confession

> sometimes hopes are scary
> but necessary to keep you alive
> -hope

Amrit decided he had to confess his feelings, regardless of the outcome. He called Ruh, his voice trembling as he said, "Ruh, ek baat kehni hai tumse."

Ruh's response was gentle and understanding. "Kaho, Amrit. Apne dil ki baat keh do." With her encouragement, he poured out his feelings, admitting his liking for her and his desire to meet and express them further.

Ruh admitted to genuinely caring about him but pointed out the financial strain and other complications. "Jab tak kismat humein milne ka mauka nahi deti, tab tak wait and whenever we'll meet you can say further," she said, leaving Amrit with a glimmer of hope.

Their conversation left Amrit with mixed emotions. On one hand, he was relieved to have finally expressed his feelings. On the other hand, he was anxious about the uncertainty of their future. But Ruh's words gave him hope, and he clung to that hope as he navigated the challenges ahead.

Amrit began to focus on his career, determined to build a stable future for himself. He wanted to be in a position where he could offer Ruh the stability and security she deserved. He worked hard, channeling his energy into his job and future plans.

> inside my head lives a dream of us
>
> it's beautiful
>
> it's scary
>
> i see it every day and night
>
> us wanting each other
>
> -dream

CHAPTER 8
The Stars & Moons

you made me homesick
for the home i never had
let it be a dream
a dream which is complete
complete with you;

Amrit's hope blossomed. He began to envision a future with Ruh, dedicating himself to his new job with renewed energy. He started writing more poems for her, a habit from his teenage years, and Ruh noticed and appreciated his efforts.

However, personal challenges led Amrit to a major decision: he decided to switch to entrepreneurship, leaving his job and city to return to his hometown. Coincidentally, Ruh got a job in the very city Amrit was leaving. It seemed destiny was playing a cruel trick on them.

Determined to express his feelings, Amrit decided to flew to Ruh's city. Nervous anticipation filled him as he planned his confession down to the last detail.

> tere dar har khwaab chhor aaya
> tujhe khwaab se haqiqat banane aaya
> tujhse mohabbat karne aaya
> jis ishq ki to haqdaar hai
> mere har khwaab ke sukh
> ko daon pe laga tujhe paane aaya

CHAPTER 9
The Meeting

> tujhe dekhna aur
> sab bhul jana
> aksar yahi hota hai
> tujhme mai aisa kho jata
> maano tu samne hai par mere khwabon me hai
> -adhuri aas

Determined to express his feelings in person, Amrit decided to visit Ruh's city before making his move. The anticipation of seeing her again filled him with both excitement and nervousness.

He meticulously planned his confession, envisioning every detail of their meeting. He wanted everything to be perfect, a moment that would reflect the depth of his feelings.

On the day of his visit, Amrit's heart raced as he boarded the flight. His mind was a whirlwind of thoughts, but his determination remained steadfast. He landed in Ruh's city with a sense of purpose, taking a taxi to a small park where he had planned to meet her.

As he waited for Ruh, memories of their journey together flooded his mind. He recalled their late-night conversations, the laughter they shared, and the silent support they offered each other during difficult times.

These memories strengthened his resolve, reminding him of the bond they had built over the years.

Finally, Ruh arrived. Watching her approach, Amrit's heart pounded with anticipation.

She looked as radiant as ever, her presence instantly calming his nerves. They embraced, and for a moment, the world around them faded away. It was just the two of them, sharing a connection that transcended time and space.

They decided to have tea at a nearby tea shop, the familiar setting providing a sense of comfort. They sipped their tea in comfortable silence, occasionally exchanging glances that spoke volumes.

Amrit wanted to seize the moment, but he also wanted to honor the significance of their meeting.

Afterward, they walked to the cafe, Ruh casually mentioned her mother's desire for her to get married soon and her own wish to settle down in a few years.

He knew this was his chance to tell Ruh everything, to lay bare his heart and soul. Amrit planned to take her to the park afterward and confess his love.

But just as he was about to speak, Ruh received an urgent call. An emergency had come up, and she had to leave abruptly.

Amrit gave a small gift along with his handwritten note which he brought with him to gift her.

They hugged goodbye, the unfinished conversation hanging in the air like an unresolved melody.

Amrit watched her go, his heart sinking with frustration and regret. He had been so close to expressing his feelings, yet the moment had slipped away.

> kuch baaten ankahi reh gayi
>
> kuch baaten ansuni reh gayin
>
> haalat ko shayad ye manzoor na tha
>
> shayad abhi kuch waqt aur tha
>
> dil aur bechain hota gaya
>
> sukoon ki khoj me
>
> sil dard dhund gaya
>
> -dard

CHAPTER 10
The Last Call

> effort
> there's no end of putting it
> jab kisi se ishq ho
> apna sari jaan laga do use paane ko
> bhale wo mile ya na
> tum haar jao par tumhara ishq jeetna chahiye
> -efforts

Frustration gnawed at Amrit as he reached the airport. Regret twisted in his gut. He decided to make one final attempt to express his feelings before his flight.

Taking a deep breath, he dialled her number. As soon as she answered, he blurted out, "Hey Ruh, mujhe tumse kuch kehna tha, aur mujhe afsos hai ki maine itna der kar diya."

Ruh's voice held a hint of amusement. "Maine intezaar kiya tha ki tum apne dil ki baat kehoge," she said.

"Aaj mujhe laga tha ki tum keh doge, Kya tumhe kisi dost ne yeh nahi sikhaya?"

Amrit chuckled nervously, "Nahi, main tumhe park le jana chahta tha, par waqt nikal gaya. Ab, is sheher mein khade hokar, airport ke andar, mujhe kehna hai: **Main tumse pyar karta hoon. Dil se**. Main apni zindagi tumhare saath bitana chahta hoon. Tum hi meri saathi ho."

A pause hung in the air. Then, Ruh spoke. "Aage bolo, Amrit. Yeh tumhara pal hai."

"Hamara," he countered, his voice thick with emotion. He poured his heart out to Ruh, describing the journey of his feelings for her—from a spark of attraction to a deep and abiding love. He confessed to crying the night he learned about her breakup, emphasizing that all he ever wanted was to see a smile on her face.

He laid bare his heart, every emotion exposed, how he used to manifest and day dream about them together, how he want her to succeed in her career and how he wants to be the pillar behind her to support her in each and every situation.

How she is a fighter and fought all the tough situation alone, and he wants to be with her in those difficult times, how he adore her mindset how he adore everything about her, how her one message used to make his day, her all the best was all he needed in the tough situations, it's something Amrit can never put into words how he felt about Ruh.

As he was expressing his emotions, the final boarding call echoed through the airport: "Last call for Mr. Amrit."

Ruh's reply was soft but determined: "Main tumhe jaldi jawab doongi!"

>tera meri zindagi me aana khaas hai
>
>mera tujhse sada ke liye
>
>mohabbat karna khas hai
>
>khas tu hai khas meri mohabbat hai
>
>pata nahi is kahani ka anjam kya hai?
>
>-intazar

CHAPTER 11
Awaiting Destiny

> tere khayalon me fir kho gaya
> tere intazar me fir so gaya
> tu haan kar ya naa kar
> mai tere mohabbat me fir dub gaya
> -love

Amrit boarded the plane with a sense of relief and anticipation. His heart was lighter for having confessed his feelings, and he knew he had done all he could.

As the plane took off, he reflected on his journey, the transformation through his love for Ruh, and the hope that now filled his heart.

He didn't know what Ruh's answer would be, but he felt a sense of peace. The future was uncertain, but he was ready to face it, knowing that he had finally expressed his true feelings. No matter what happened, he believed in the power of love and the resilience it had given him.

मुझे तेरी मोहब्बत की तक़रीबन पता है,
पर मुझे मेरे इश्क़ की सुद्धत भी पता है!
तुम मेरी हो या मैं तुम्हारा,
ये मैं न जानु
मैं तो बस इतना जानु
इस मोहब्बत को अमर कर,
एक धागी में पिरो कर हमेशा अपने दिल के पास रखूँ!!

ज़रूरी नहीं कि हर कहानी का अंत हो,
कभी कभी कुछ कहानियों को एक खूबसूरत मोड़ दे देनी चाहिए,
एक अधूरी खूबसूरत feeling - प्यार जो शब्द ही अधूरा है,
बस इस कहानी की तरह!!

About the Author

Harsh Gupta

~ Someone who pens life into stories to make it the art it deserves to be.

> you tell me
> to forget it and move on
> i don't know how to unfeel love
> once i have felt it?

www.ingramcontent.com/pod-product-compliance
Lightning Source LLC
LaVergne TN
LVHW041642070526
838199LV00053B/3518